To my brothers and sisters

Cynthia, Jay, Roger,

Daniel, Carolyn, and Leo

Four Valentines in a Rainstorm

FELICIA BOND

THOMAS Y. CROWELL   NEW YORK

Library of Congress Cataloging in Publication Data
Bond, Felicia.
Four valentines in a rainstorm.
Summary: On the day it rains hearts, Cornelia
Augusta makes Valentine cards for four of her friends.
[1. Valentine's Day—Fiction.   2. Valentines
—Fiction]   I. title.   II. Title: 4 valentines
in a rainstorm.
PZ7.B63666Fo 1983   [E]   82-45586
ISBN 0-690-04307-4 (lib. bdg.)
ISBN 0-690-04306-6 (pbk.)

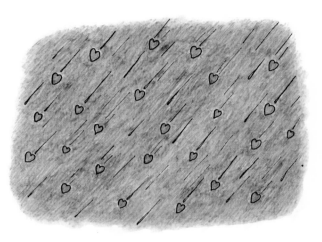

One day it started raining hearts,

and Cornelia Augusta caught one.

She caught another,

and another.

It wasn't very hard, so she caught
some more.

"It must be getting close to Valentine's
Day," she thought,

and she set to work making Valentines.
The hearts she caught would make
perfect cards.

Cornelia Augusta saw that all of her
hearts were different.

She looked at each one
from the front,
and the back,
and the side,
and decided which ones would be just
right for each of her friends.

She found seven that were more or less alike and strung them together with a needle and thread.

"I know just the person for this one," she thought.

Then Cornelia Augusta took an especially handsome heart and pasted it on a piece of paper.

In the center of the heart she glued a
cotton ball, one that was very white
and very soft. And she knew instantly
who this card would be for.

Cornelia Augusta had eight hearts left.

On the largest one she drew circles
and then very carefully cut them out.

The other hearts were *so* small, she
arranged all of them on one piece of
paper. Around the hearts she painted
patterns of many colors. Then she
folded her design in half.

There was no doubt in her mind
who would receive these.

Cornelia Augusta put a stamp on each
of her Valentines

and mailed them.

It never rained hearts again—

not where Cornelia Augusta lived,
anyway—

but it didn't matter,

because the next year,

and the next,

and all the years after that,